E
Hannert

Book design by Susan Van Horn.
Typeset in Thistlem.
The illustrations in this book were rendered in
colored pencils and markers on sandpaper.
Printed in Hong Kong.
ISBN 0-8118-2812-3

Library of Congress Cataloging-in-Publication Data
Hannert, Todd.
Morning dance / by Todd Hannert.
p. cm.
Summary: Sherman makes up a dance while brushing his teeth
which escalates into an adventurous chain of events that gives him
an unusual way of getting to the breakfast table.
ISBN 0-8118-2812-3
[1. Morning—Fiction. 2. Dance—Fiction. 3. Stories in rhyme.]
I. Title.
PZ8.3.H1948 Mo 2001
[E]--dc21
00-008943

Distributed in Canada by Raincoast Books
9050 Shaughnessy Street, Vancouver, British Columbia V6P 6E5

10 9 8 7 6 5 4 3 2 1

Chronicle Books LLC
85 Second Street, San Francisco, California 94105

www.chroniclebooks.com/Kids

Morning Dance

By Todd Hannert

chronicle books·san francisco

Every day is the same.

The same old thing
in the very same way.

But I kind of made up
a dance this morning

while I was brushing my teeth.

My mom yelled,

"Sherman, you'll be late for school!"

"Come down here now and eat!"

I'm not so sure what happened next.
I sort of bumped my toe.

My toothbrush kind of
fell out of my mouth.
And Teddy. . . I really don't know.

I made it out of the bathroom
then headed toward the stairs.

This more or less changed a bit

since I didn't quite make it there.

I went a slightly different way.
About that there is no doubt.

"Sherman, where are you?"

I heard my mom say.

"You better be up and about!"

Most days my dog
is not so quick.
In fact, he's pretty slow.

But this morning he must
have had a lot to do.
He was really on the go.

YIPPY

YO!

YIPPY

Ya!

ZIPPY

dee!

ZIPPY

dum!

Before I knew it I was at the table where my breakfast was waiting for me.

"Sherman, honey, what took you so long?
It's almost time to leave."

I'm probably not remembering it all

or exactly the way it was done.

But starting the day
with a morning dance
was sort of kind of fun.

Do Not Disturb